DATE DUE		

TELL ME ABOUT
COLOR

TELL ME ABOUT
COLOR

By ALAIN GRÉE
Pictures by GÉRARD GRÉE
Translated from the French by ALEXANDRA CHAPMAN

Library of Congress Catalog Card Number: 71-179404
ISBN: 0-448-02934-0 (Trade Edition)
ISBN: 0-448-04468-4 (Library Edition)

Translation copyright © 1972, by CASTERMAN, Paris.   Originally published in French under the title *Petit Tom Decouvre Les Couleurs,* © 1970, CASTERMAN, Paris. Published pursuant to agreement with CASTERMAN, Paris.
Not for sale in the British Commonwealth, except Canada.

GROSSET & DUNLAP • Publishers • NEW YORK
A NATIONAL GENERAL COMPANY

Tommy and his sister Susan do not go to the same school. But now and then they would like to walk home together.

"Let's plan to meet after school," suggested Tommy. "Since you get out be-fore I do, you can wait for me in the park."

The first time, Susan wore a white coat, white shoes and a white cap.

But it was winter. The ground and the

4

and the trees were green. Again, Tommy couldn't find Susan.

The third time, Susan wore dark pants, a dark coat and a dark hood.

But night was falling, and Tommy couldn't find her this time, either.

"The colors keep playing tricks on us," Tommy concluded. "I'm going to ask Mr. Barnaby, the artist, for advice."

trees in the park were covered with snow, and Tommy couldn't find Susan.

The second time, Susan wore a green skirt, green stockings and a green hat.

But it was springtime, and the grass

The children could hardly believe their eyes when they entered Mr. Barnaby's studio. Tubes of paint, brushes, and sheets of drawing paper everywhere!

"Colors are curious things," Mr. Barnaby explained. "Some are simple, others are not. Look at the simple, or primary, colors — blue, red and yellow."

"Baby chicks are yellow!" exclaimed Susan. "And cherries are red!"

"Very good," Mr. Barnaby smiled. "Do you also recognize the colors of other objects?"

The children named them, one by one.

"And now, Tommy, look carefully. I am hanging a white sheet on the white wall. Can you see it very well?"

"No," admitted Tommy.

"That's why you missed Susan the first time!"

wheat

tomato

periwinkle

milk

mimosa

fire engine

coal

chick

sea and sky

cherries

paper

snowman

forget-
me-not

crow

record

"Do you know what will happen if you mix the primary colors with one another?" asked Mr. Barnaby.

Tommy and Susan raced excitedly toward the brushes.

"May we try it, please, Mr. Barnaby?"

"Of course," the artist replied. "You will get new or secondary colors. For example, if you mix blue and yellow, you will have . . ."

"Green!" squealed Susan.

"Exactly," replied Mr. Barnaby. "Now, pay attention, Tommy. It's hard to see a green object against a green background. That's why you couldn't find Susan when she was wearing green."

8

white
+
black
=
gray

Secondary colors
When you mix
blue
and red,
you get
purple

Mr. Barnaby gathered some drawings together.

"Look," he said. "Some of these colors are bright and others are dark."

"Yellow is bright," remarked Susan.

"And purple is dark," said Tommy.

"Right!" agreed Mr. Barnaby. "But each of these colors can be brightened or darkened, just by adding white or black. As you've discovered, Tommy, it's not easy to see something dark in front of a dark background."

Mr. Cooper's house is dark,
both inside and out. Even when the sun
is shining, his house looks gloomy!
But one day the florist arrives
with many flowers.
The painters come, too.
Mr. Cooper is getting married!
The house is no longer sad.

"Colors aren't so mysterious any more," said Tommy happily. "We know that some colors are simple . . ."

"And when we mix them," added Susan, "we get secondary colors . . ."

"Some of them bright, some of them dark," finished Tommy.

"You've certainly learned something," smiled Mr. Barnaby. "Now, let's play a game."

The children clapped their hands with glee.

"All right, here's the game," said Mr. Barnaby. "There are certain plants and

animals which have the same names as colors — like oranges, the brown bear, and — can either one of you think of any others?"

"The bluebird!"

"The rose! The violet!"

"The chestnut! The redbreast!"

"Excellent!" beamed Mr. Barnaby. "Now can you think of some colors which have the names of plants or objects, like cherry red or bottle green?"

"Lemon yellow!"

"Apple green! Olive green!"

"Chocolate brown! Lilac pink!"

Mr. Barnaby raised his hand for silence. "We are forgetting one important detail, children," he said.

Tommy and Susan looked puzzled.

"It's true that there are animals, plants and things of one particular color, but there are also those which have many different colors — like parrots, and butterflies, and tropical fish — and even the rainbow!"

"I remember Christmas Eve, when we decorated the tree with ornaments of every color," said Tommy. "It was just beautiful!"

Tommy has fun playing
in his Indian costume.
"Peek-a-boo, I see you!"
he calls to Susan.
"Bet you can't find me!"
   "I see your feathers!" laughs Susan.
"If it's not you hiding behind
that chair, it's the parrot!"

"Mr. Barnaby," asked Tommy, "if I know what color clothes Susan is wearing, won't I be able a choose a meeting-place where I could see her?"

"Perhaps, Tommy. But you couldn't be sure, because objects can change color. Sometimes it takes several years,

and sometimes only a few minutes."

"I don't understand," said Tommy. "How can that happen?"

The artist brought out several canvases. "See all the things I've painted," he said. "As you can see, nature often changes her color."

the leaves of trees . . .

. . . as the seasons change

skin and hair . . .

. . . with sun and age

the lobster . . .

. . . after cooking

a country scene . . .

. . . covered with snow

the sky and the sea . . .

. . . in stormy weather

and all objects . . .

. . . in the dark

"But, Mr. Barnaby, if colors play tricks on us so often, are they really necessary?"

"Of course, Tommy," the artist replied. "For instance, certain colors mean certain things to us, like the red of the stoplight, or the yellow lines on the street where people may cross from sidewalk to sidewalk. Because of these familiar colors, a great many traffic accidents never happen."

He continued. "Look out of the window. You'll find even more examples of colors that tell us things and perform a service."

"The red cross of the ambulance!"

"The soldiers' uniforms!"

"The colors of the flags!"

"The uniforms of the ballplayers!"

"See? There's no end to it!" said Mr. Barnaby. "Let's take a picture!"

Click!

A few minutes later, Mr. Barnaby returned with the snapshot.

"Oh, it's black-and-white," said Tommy, disappointed. "Everything seems to look the same."

"Well, then, Tommy, you can see that without color life is less exciting. For this reason, too, colors are useful—they decorate nature and our houses and everything around us."

One day all of the crayons and colored pencils held a meeting.

Green Crayon was the first to speak. "I'm tired of coloring lettuce and grass and peas and water," he said. "There must be more to color."

"At least you have a few things to color," said White Crayon. "Lately I've been coloring nothing but snowmen."

"I know just how you feel," said Black Crayon. "I've had nothing but coal to color."

"I've been coloring tomatoes," said Red Crayon.

"And I," sighed Blue Crayon, "have been coloring nothing but the sky and the sea. I feel so blue!"

"Can't we just change things?"

leek   lettuce   tea   snowman   tomato

"Mr. Barnaby," asked Tommy as they left the studio, "how can I be sure of finding Susan next time?"

"Well, now, let's see," said Mr. Barnaby thoughtfully. "Why not have her wait for you right by the school door—and call out your name as soon as she sees you?"

And that's exactly what Tommy did!

asked Pink Pencil. "I'm sure it would make life more interesting for all of us."

The crayons and the pencils put their pointed heads together—and agreed that that was a splendid idea.

Now, if you want to see what can happen when crayons and colored pencils choose to color whatever they like, look at the pictures below!

sea and sky

coal